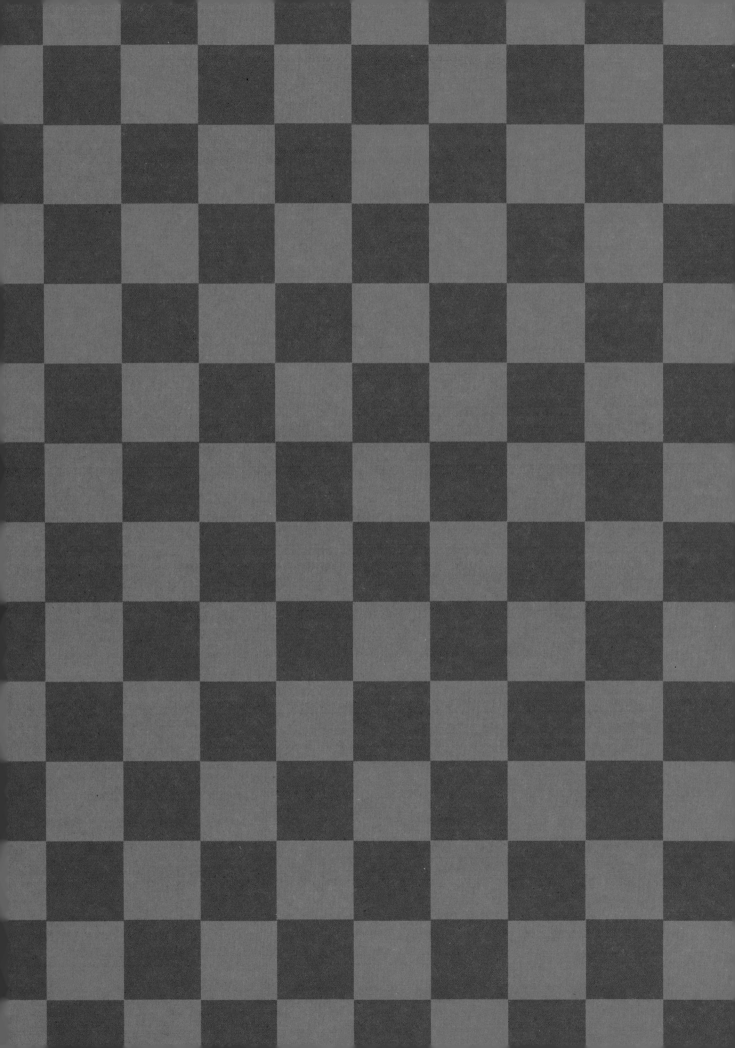

Disney

A Very Merry Memory Book

Text by Sharee Hopler

Interior Book Design by Alfred Giuliani

One Hundred and One Dalmatians copyright © 1961 Disney Enterprises, Inc. Based on the book *The Hundred and One Dalmatians* by Dodie Smith, published by The Viking Press
Monsters, Inc. copyright © 2001 Disney Enterprises, Inc./Pixar Animation Studios
Toy Story 2 copyright © 1999 Disney Enterprises, Inc./Pixar Animation Studios
Original *Toy Story* Elements copyright © Disney Enterprises, Inc. All rights reserved.
Winnie the Pooh characters based on the "Winnie the Pooh" works by A. A. Milne and E. H. Shepard

Printed in the United States of America

ISBN 0-7868-3494-3

Library of Congress Catalog Card Number: 2004103806

First Edition

10 9 8 7 6 5 4 3 2 1

For more Disney Press fun, visit www.disneybooks.com

Disney

A Very Merry Memory Book

Written by _____
(your name here)

Drawings by _____
(your name here)

Disney PRESS

NEW YORK

Hi, boys and girls!

Christmas is my favorite time of the year. It means a smooch from Minnie under the mistletoe, Daisy's delicious Christmas cookies, tree trimming with the gang, and lots of other swell holiday fun. Use this book to write about all *your* special Christmas memories. In some places, you will be asked to select answers that best describe how you celebrate the holidays. Put a star sticker from the back of this book next to the answer of your choice. When you are finished, you'll have your very own Christmas memory book!

MICKEY MOUSE

Let's start by finding out all about *you*. . . .

All About Me!

Today is _____.
(month/day/year)

There are _____ days left until Christmas!

I am _____ years old.

I am _____ feet _____ inches tall.

I have _____ eyes.
(color)

I have _____ hair.
(color)

Here is a picture
of me.

(Paste photo here.)

I live at _____ .

(address)

Here's a picture I drew of my house decorated for Christmas!

My Family

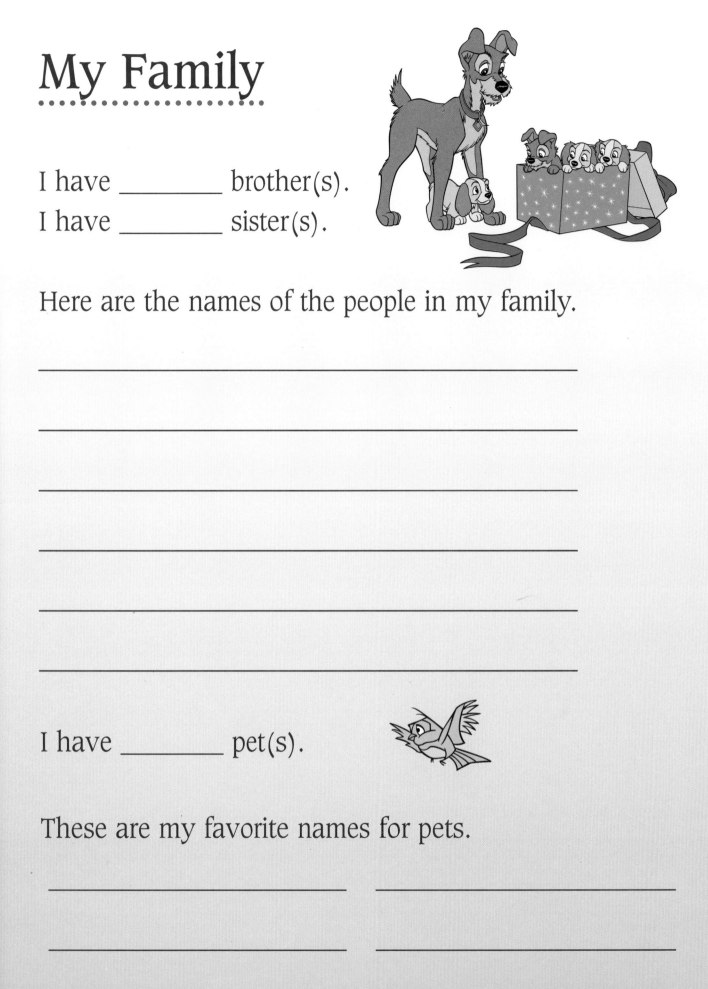

I have _____ brother(s).

I have _____ sister(s).

Here are the names of the people in my family.

_____

_____

_____

_____

_____

I have _____ pet(s).

These are my favorite names for pets.

_____   _____

_____   _____

Place a star sticker from the back of the book next to the kind of pet(s) you have or would like to have.

⭐ Cat   ⭐ Lizard   ⭐ Fish

⭐ Dog   ⭐ Hamster   ⭐ Rabbit

⭐ Other _____

Here's a picture of my family and me.

(Paste photo here.)

Countdown to Christmas!

Place a number sticker from the sticker pages in the back of the book to count the days till Christmas.

My Christmas Firsts

I just can't wait till Christmas!

Christmas is coming, and you can see, hear, and smell the signs of the most wonderful season of all.

First decorations I saw _____

First song I heard _____

First Christmas smell _____

You will need:

- A grown-up's help
- Construction paper
- A stapler
- Scissors

Directions:

🎁 With your grown-up's help, cut out 25 strips of construction paper in various colors. Each strip should be approximately 8½ inches long and 1½ inches wide.

🎁 Staple one strip into a loop.

🎁 Take another strip and slip it through the first loop and make a second loop. Staple.

🎁 Continue to add strips and make loops until you've completed the chain.

🎁 Beginning December 1, take one loop off each day until it's Christmas Day!

A-Christmas-Tree-Hunting
We Will Go!

My family gets our Christmas tree at _____
_____ .

Here's a picture I drew of the perfect Christmas tree.

My Christmas Tree

(Use your star stickers from the back of the book.)

Here's how my family decorates our tree.

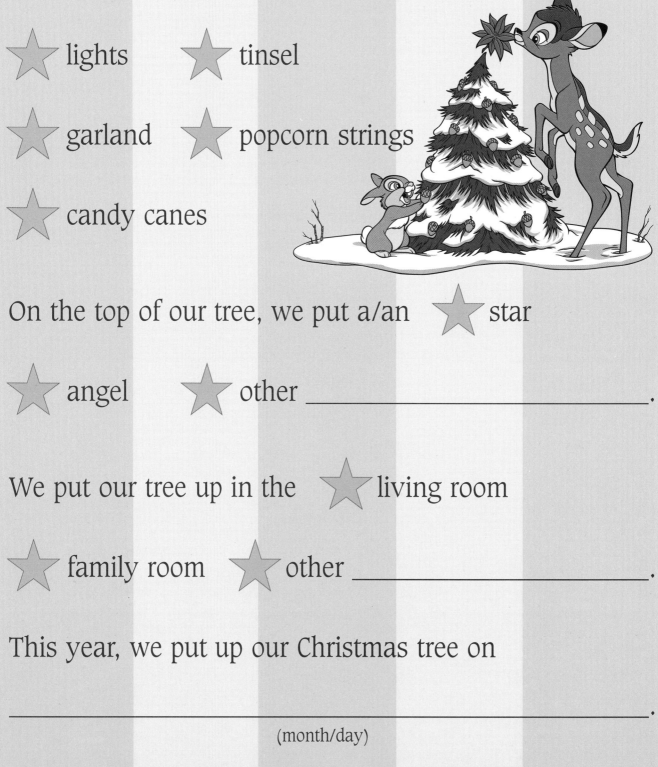

⭐ lights   ⭐ tinsel

⭐ garland   ⭐ popcorn strings

⭐ candy canes

On the top of our tree, we put a/an ⭐ star

⭐ angel   ⭐ other _____.

We put our tree up in the ⭐ living room

⭐ family room   ⭐ other _____.

This year, we put up our Christmas tree on

_____.

(month/day)

The oldest ornament is _____.

The newest ornament is _____.

My favorite ornament is _____.

It is special to me because _____

_____.

Here's a picture I drew of it.

Can you imagine how some of your favorite Disney friends might decorate their own trees? Would Belle decorate with candles, plates, cups and saucers, and silverware? Perhaps Ariel would trim her tree with seashells, sand dollars, and sea stars.

Using crayons, markers, pencils, and stickers, you can decorate these trees the way you think Winnie the Pooh and Mickey might. There are some stickers at the back of this book to get you started.

Deck the Halls!

(Use your star stickers from the back of the book.)

Here's how my family decorates our house inside and out.

⭐ lights

⭐ candles

⭐ candy canes

⭐ mistletoe

⭐ wreaths

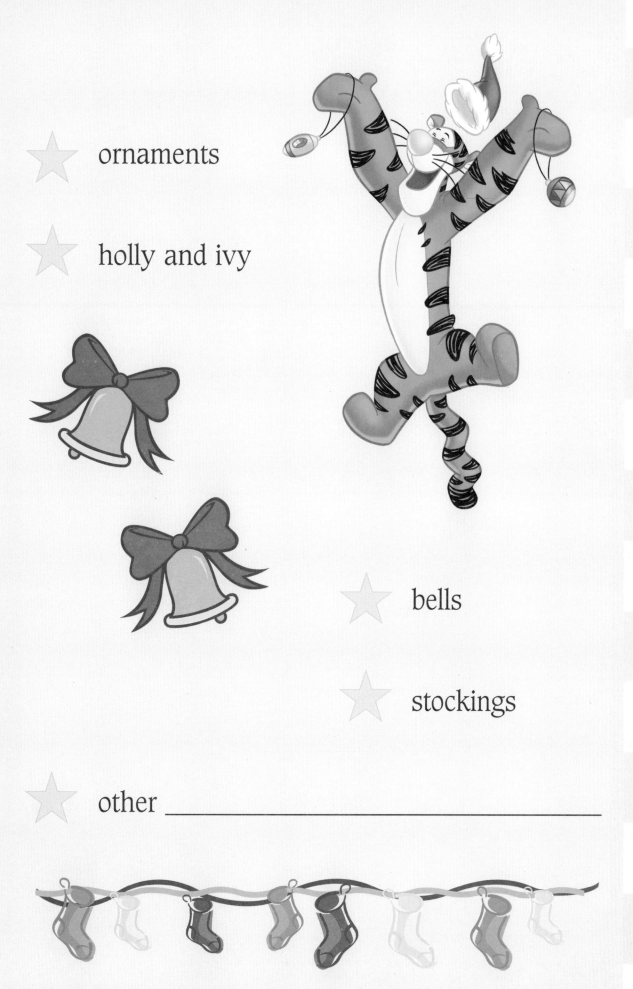

☆ ornaments

☆ holly and ivy

☆ bells

☆ stockings

☆ other _____

Here's a picture I drew of my stocking.

Here's a wreath I decorated.

Presents!

My Wish List

_____

_____

_____

_____

_____

_____

_____

_____

My "Need to Get a Gift For" List

Person	Gift Idea	Got it!
		☐
		☐
		☐
		☐
		☐
		☐
		☐
		☐
		☐
		☐

Fill in the blanks to finish the Christmas story of two elves, Tinsel and Bulb, who are trying to think of the perfect gift for Santa.

The Perfect Gift

*O*nce upon a Christmastime, two of Santa's elves, Tinsel and Bulb, were trying to decide what to give Santa for Christmas. They'd had a lot of ideas; coming up with ideas wasn't the problem—choosing the perfect gift was.

"We could give him _____," said Tinsel.
(article of clothing)

"No, no, he already has a great many of those," said Bulb. "And besides we gave him a _____
(same article of clothing)
last year. How about a _____ or a
(animal)
_____? Now, that's something
(toy)
he could really use."

"Good, yes," said Tinsel, "but not _____
(a word that describes something)

26

enough. We want to give Santa the perfect Christmas

gift. Nothing too _____ or
                      (color)

_____, but just right."
        (size)

   And so it went between the elves, back and forth,

forth and back, for about _____ hours.
                               (number)

Finally, both Tinsel and Bulb threw up their

_____ and yelled, "_____!"
   (part of the body, plural)   (exclamation)

   "We must come to a decision, and quick," said Bulb.

"Christmas is just around the _____, and
                                    (place)

time is running out. We've got to put our

_____ together and come up with
   (part of the body, plural)

something _____."
           (a word that describes something)

   Well, Tinsel and Bulb did indeed put their

_____ together and stayed that way for
   (same part of the body, plural)

another _____ hours. They became very
              (number)

tired; their eyes _____, and their
                       (action word)

(Story continues on next page)

_____ hurt from all the effort they were
(part of the body, plural)

putting into coming up with the perfect Christmas gift

for Santa.

   Finally, it was Christmas Eve

and Tinsel and Bulb, try as they

might, couldn't stay awake for another

_____ longer. They fell asleep on the
(measure of time)

_____ with _____ smiles
(piece of furniture)   (a word that describes something)

on their faces. Santa found them this way, asleep by

the Christmas tree. He smiled, then

_____, and then laughed
(action word ending in -ed)

out loud until _____ ran down his
(thing)

_____ cheeks, and his sides ached.
(a word that describes something)

   "Ahh, me," Santa said, when at last his guffaws

subsided to giggles, and he had wiped his tears and

blown his _____ nose. "Tinsel and Bulb
(a word that describes something)

have given me the best present in the world—the gift of laughter. And people wonder why I'm so jolly. These elves crack me up!"

With a final chuckle, Santa set out to deliver to children around the world the gifts of happiness, delight, surprise, wonder, and, yes, best of all, laughter.

It's a Wrap!

Here are some creative ideas for wrapping gifts:

- newspaper, especially the colorful comics section
- large pieces of scrap fabric
- take-out menus
- drawings and paintings brought home from school

 **Make your own wrapping paper!**

You will need:

- A grown-up's help
- 1 fine-tip marker, black
- Compressed sponges
- Scissors
- 1 roll of kraft paper
- Nontoxic water-based paint (red, green, and any other colors of your choice)
- Plastic plates for the paints

Directions:

● Draw simple holiday designs such as stockings, stars, and candy canes on sponges with a felt-tip pen.

● With your grown-up's help, cut out the designs with your scissors. Wet the sponges until they expand and let them dry.

● Spread the kraft paper out on a table. If it doesn't lie flat, weigh the edges down with cans of food or similar objects.

● Put each color paint on a different plastic plate.

● Gently dip one of the sponges into the paint.

● Press the sponge onto the paper. Then carefully lift it up and press it down again in another place on the paper. Repeat, adding paint to the sponge as needed.

● Cover the paper with as many sponge prints as you like, using many different shapes and colors.

Once your paper dries, it's time to wrap and decorate! Don't forget to use the gift tag stickers at the back of this book!

(Use your star stickers from the back of the book.)

My family and I exchange gifts on

⭐ Christmas Eve   ⭐ Christmas morning

⭐ Other _____.

My all-time favorite gift that I got was _____

_____.

My all-time favorite gift that I gave was _____

_____.

 **Can you keep a Christmas secret?**

Be a "Secret Santa" by doing something nice for someone else, but don't let him or her know that it was you!

Here's a picture of my family and me exchanging gifts last Christmas.

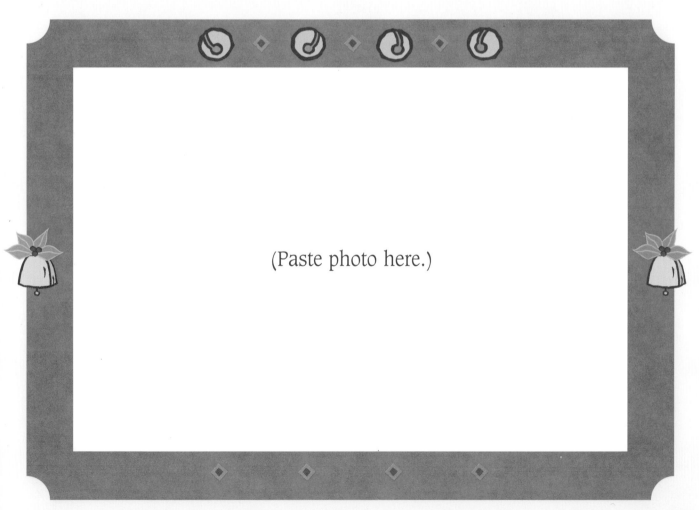

(Paste photo here.)

Christmas Tails

Here are some ways to help your animal friends celebrate Christmas.

 Bake dog biscuits in bone shapes.

Dog Biscuits Baked with Love

You will need:
- A grown-up's help
- 2 cups unbleached wheat flour
- 1 cup cornmeal
- Pinch of salt
- 1 egg
- 3 tablespoons vegetable oil
- 2 teaspoons chopped fresh parsley
- $^3/_4$ cup chicken broth

Directions:

🥁 Ask a grown-up to preheat the oven to 400°F.

🥁 Mix the flour, cornmeal, and salt in one bowl.

🥁 In a separate and larger bowl, whip the egg with the oil, parsley, and chicken broth. Add the flour mixture and mix until a soft dough forms.

🥁 Knead the dough and roll it out to a ½-inch thickness. Use cookie cutters to cut the dough into shapes.

🥁 Bake for 15 minutes. Cool the biscuits before serving.

🐾 Have a Christmas picture taken of your pets. (You may want to use this next year for your Christmas cards.)

🐾 Hang ornaments with your pet's name or picture on the Christmas tree.

🐾 Make garlands of cranberries and popcorn for wildlife and hang on trees and bushes.

🐾 Change your pet's everyday collar and leash for something with a holiday theme.

🐾 Decorate the outside of your pet's cage or tank in a holiday theme.

🐾 Give your pet a special treat to eat on Christmas Day.

🐾 Other ideas _____

_____

_____

Caroling

Tips for successful and cheerful Christmas caroling:

♪ Decide what your group will sing and whose houses you will go to.

♪ Bring copies of the carols that will be sung.

♪ If you will be caroling at night, use flashlights and bring a grown-up.

♪ Have fun!

♪ Be sure to record your Christmas caroling memories!

We visited these houses: _____

_____

_____

We sang these songs: _____

_____

_____

These are the names of the people I caroled with:

_____

_____

We started caroling at _____.
(time)

We finished caroling at _____.
(time)

Here is a photo of me and my fellow carolers.

(Paste photo here.)

It's the Most Wonderful Time of the School Year!

My friends celebrate Christmas by _____

_____

_____.

My friends celebrate other winter holidays by _____

_____

_____.

My school is decorated with _____

_____

_____.

Here are some special things that go on at my school in the weeks before Christmas.

(Use your star stickers from the back of the book.)

⭐ Holiday concert

⭐ Holiday play or pageant

⭐ Food collection for a local food bank

⭐ A visit from Santa Claus

⭐ Class party

Plan Your Own Christmas Extravaganza!

Design an invitation.

(Be sure to make an extra one for the memory envelope in the back of the book!)

Songs I will sing:_____

_____

Other performers:_____

_____

The following costumes will be needed:_____

_____

Intermission will be _____ minutes long.

The following refreshments will be served:_____

_____

Sample invitation:

Presenting...

My Very Own Christmas Spectacular!

Starring

_____

&

_____

Time:_____

Date:_____

Place:_____

Refreshments will be served during intermission.

If you see only one show this Christmas season, make sure it's mine!

Gingerbread Houses!

If I lived in a gingerbread house . . .

The roof would be decorated with_____.

The windows would be_____.

The walls would be covered with_____.

The door would be_____.

The chimney would be decorated with_____.

The snow outside would be made of_____.

44

Here's a story I wrote about a gingerbread family that lives in a gingerbread house.

_____

_____

_____

_____

_____

_____

_____

Christmas Cup of Cheer

Write down 12 holiday activities on 12 small pieces of paper. Fold each piece of paper into a tiny square and put all 12 into your designated Christmas Cup of Cheer (this can be any type of container, box, or cup). Each day, pull out one slip of paper and perform that holiday activity. You may use the activities provided on the next few pages or replace them with your own special ideas.

1   Hang some mistletoe.

2   Cut out a paper snowflake to hang on a window or door.

You will need:
- A grown-up's help
- White paper
- Scissors

Directions:

Fold a piece of 8½ x 11-inch paper in half.

Fold over one side as shown, then the other.

With your grown-up's help, cut off the edges of the paper in an arc, as shown.

Cut triangles, squares, and other shapes out of each side, being careful not to cut completely across.

Unfold your snowflake and tape it onto a window or door.

3 **Share a cup of hot chocolate with someone you love.**

Make Your Own Hot Cocoa Mix

(Enough mix for about 20 cups)

You will need:

- A grown-up's help
- $1\frac{2}{3}$ cups nonfat dry milk powder
- 1 cup confectioners' sugar
- $\frac{1}{3}$ cup unsweetened cocoa powder
- $\frac{1}{2}$ teaspoon salt

Directions:

Measure the ingredients into a plastic container or a clean, empty coffee can.

Cover and shake until well mixed.

When you're ready for a cup, put 4 heaping teaspoons of the cocoa mixture into a mug. With the help of a grown-up, add boiling water and stir until the powder dissolves.

4 **Read a Christmas story to a younger sibling or friend.**

My favorite Christmas story is _____

_____.

Here's a scene I drew from it.

5 Donate toys you no longer play with to a shelter.

6 Watch your favorite Christmas special on television, video, or DVD with a friend.

Some other Christmas specials I enjoy are _____

_____

_____.

They are my favorites because_____

_____

_____.

7 **Sing along with a favorite Christmas tape or CD.**

My favorite Christmas song is _____

_____.

Some of my other favorite carols are_____

_____

_____

_____

_____.

8 **Walk or drive around your town or neighborhood to see the decorations.**

9 **Watch a Christmas movie you've never seen before.**

My favorite Christmas movie of all time is

_____ .

Draw a character from this movie.

10 **Make Christmas cards for your classmates and teacher.**

Paste one of your cards below.

(Paste card here.)

11 Bake cookies and decorate them. Package a dozen for a neighbor and don't forget to set aside a few for Santa.

My favorite cookie is _____

_____.

Here are some cookies I decorated for Christmas.

Write your favorite cookie recipe in the space provided.

THE BEST COOKIE EVER

12 **Write a letter to Santa!**

Dear Santa,

From Your Friend,

Outdoor Fun!

(Use your star stickers from the back of the book.)

During the holiday season,
I love to:

⭐ Go sledding

⭐ Go snowshoeing

⭐ Build a
snowperson

Have snowball
fights

Go ice fishing

Go ice-skating

Snowboard/ski

Other _____

Build a Snowperson!

How would you decorate a snowperson? Would you decorate it in a traditional way with a carrot, buttons, coal, and a broom, or would you go wacky with old CDs, tennis balls, a guitar, and a snorkel?

Draw a picture of your snowperson, and then write a story about him or her on the following page.

_____

_____

_____

_____

_____

_____

_____

_____

_____

_____

"Santa Claus"—Around the World!

Dun Che Lao Ren ("Christmas Old Man")—China

Père Noël—France

Weihnachtsmann ("Christmas Man")—Germany

Kanakaloka—Hawaii

Babbo Natale—Italy

Julenissen ("Christmas Gnome")—Norway

Ded Moroz ("Grandfather Frost")—Russia

Jultomten ("Christmas Brownie")—Sweden

Father Christmas— United Kingdom

A Trip to See Santa

I visited Santa on _____.
                        (month/day)

I visited him at_____

_____.

I had to wait on line for _____ minutes.

I told him _____

_____

_____.

(Use your star stickers from the back of the book.)

⭐   Mrs. Claus was there, too.

⭐   Elves were there, too.

64

Here's a photo of Santa and me.

(Paste photo here.)

Candy Cane Fun!

You can do lots of things with candy canes:

🍬 You can use one to stir your hot chocolate.

🍬 You can hang several on your Christmas tree.

🍬 You can glue two candy canes together in the center, facing each other, to make a "sweet heart" for your teacher.

🍬 You can make a reindeer ornament for a friend, following the directions below.

Reindeer Candy Cane Ornament

You will need:

- A grown-up's help
- 1 individually wrapped, 6-inch candy cane
- Craft glue
- 1 very small red or brown pom-pom
- 2 5-mm wiggle eyes
- 1 ribbon (approximately 8 inches long)
- 2 18-inch colored pipe cleaners
- Scissors

Directions:

🍃 Glue pom-pom onto the end of candy cane hook. This will be the nose of the reindeer.

🍃 Glue eyes onto the candy cane just above the nose.

🍃 Tie ribbon into a bow on the straight part of the candy cane.

🍃 Wrap one pipe cleaner around the crook of the candy cane and begin to shape the antlers.

🍃 With your grown-up's help, cut the second pipe cleaner in half.

🍃 Tie or wrap one of the pipe cleaner halves to the right antler.

🍃 Tie or wrap the second pipe cleaner half to the left antler.

🍃 Bend the pipe cleaners until they look like antlers.

Fill in the Christmas alphabet.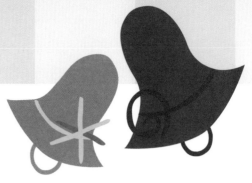

A   angel

B   bells

C   cookies

D   _____

E   _____

F   _____

G   _____

H   _____

I   _____

J   _____

K   _____

L   _____

M   _____

N _____

O _____

P _____

Q _____

R _____

S _____

T _____

U _____

V _____

W _____

X _____

Y _____

Z _____

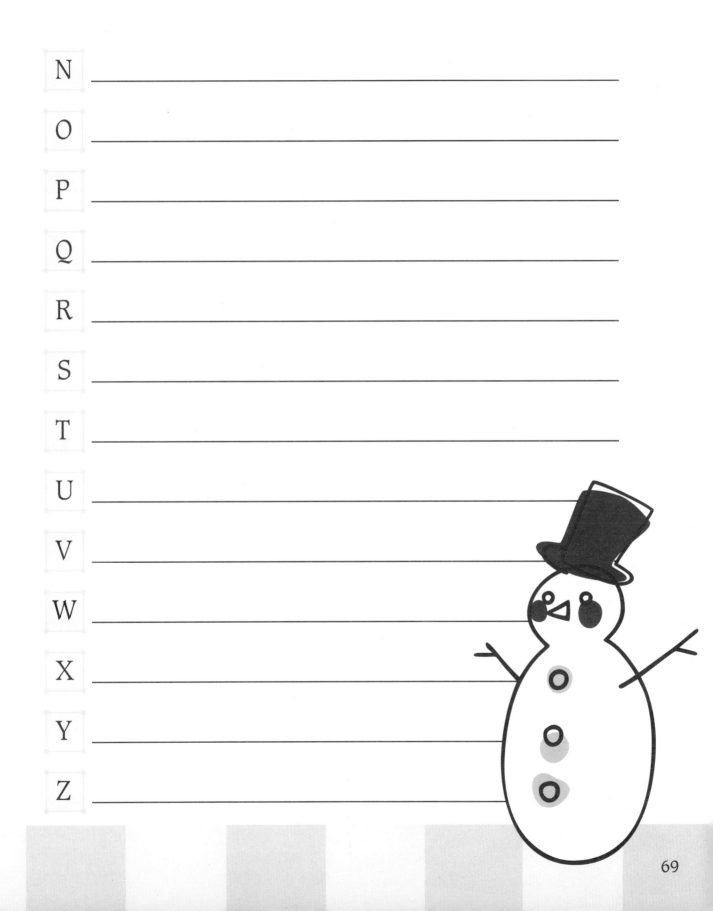

Christmas Past

Here are some of my favorite photos of my family and me from past Christmases.

(Paste photo here.)

(Paste photo here.)

(Paste photo here.)

Here's what happened on my favorite Christmas Eve ever.

_____

_____

_____

_____

Here's what happened on my favorite Christmas ever.

_____

_____

_____

_____

Ask an older relative what they remember about their own Christmas celebrations when they were younger and write their memories below.

Name _____

What was the best present you ever got? _____

_____

What was the best present you ever gave? _____

_____

What did you eat for Christmas dinner? _____

_____

Did you have a Christmas tree? _____

Was it large or small? _____

Who did you celebrate Christmas with? _____

_____

_____

_____

Santa Snacks

I like to leave these snacks for Santa: _____

_____

_____

I like to leave these snacks for his reindeer: _____

_____

_____

This year I will leave: _____

_____

_____

If you were Santa, what snack would you like to have waiting for you? Draw a picture of it.

Christmas Dinner

Here are the foods my family and I will be enjoying this Christmas dinner. (Don't forget dessert and drinks, and put a star from the back of the book beside your favorite food!)

Here's a picture of my family and me
at Christmas dinner.

(Paste photo here.)

Here's a list of who was there.

_____

_____

_____

_____

Christmas Cards

(Use your star stickers from the back of the book.)

My family and I ⭐ send ⭐ do not send

Christmas cards.

This is how we display the ones we receive: _____

_____.

Our first card came from _____.

It arrived on _____.

The Christmas card that traveled the farthest
distance to get to us was from _____

_____.

The Christmas card that traveled the shortest
distance to get to us was from _____

_____.

(Paste your favorite Christmas card here.)

After you've finished displaying your Christmas cards, don't forget to save them in the envelope at the back of your memory book!

Christmas Day!

(Use your star stickers from the back of the book.)

I woke up at _____.
(time)

 I was the first person awake in our house.

I wasn't, but _____ was.

Santa and his reindeer ate   all   some

none   of the snacks we left them.

82

The first gift I opened was _____

_____.

Here's a drawing of the face I made when I opened it.

My favorite gift this year was _____

_____ .

Here's a picture I drew of it.

My favorite gift that I gave this year was _____

_____.

The biggest gift I got this year was _____

_____.

Here's a list of what was in my stocking.

_____

_____

_____

_____

The first toy I played with was _____

_____.

"Merry Christmas"— Around the World!

Glædelig Jul—Danish

Joyeux Noël—French

Hyvää Joulua—Finnish

Mele Kalikimaka—Hawaiian

Sungtan Chukha—Korean

Buon Natale—Italian

Srozhdestovm Kristovim—Russian

Feliz Navidad—Spanish

Krismasi njema—Swahili

Suksun Wan Christmas—Thai

Fröhliche Weihnachten—German

Nadolig Llawen—
Welsh

Kala Christouyenna—Greek

Christmas Keepsakes

Here are some Christmas treasures you can add to the envelope at the back of the book:

- A gift tag
- A ticket stub from a movie, concert, or play
- A piece of ribbon

just 4 you!

- A piece of wrapping paper
- Your favorite Christmas card

- The program from a concert or play

- Newspaper or magazine clippings about the holiday season

- A family Christmas newsletter

Sweets
for
my
Sweet

JOY

- An invitation to a holiday party

Here are some of my favorite photos from the holiday season. Add a caption in the line provided under each photo.

(Paste photo here.)

(Paste photo here.)

(Paste photo here.)

Here's a picture I drew of my favorite Disney character celebrating Christmas.

My Thank-You-Note List

This year I will need to write to:

Plans for the New Year

Here is how I'll spend New Year's Eve. _____

_____

_____

_____

_____

In the New Year, I wish for

_____

_____

_____

_____.

Happy New Year

_____ !

(Write year here.)

Stickers for **Countdown to Christmas** calendar:

Stickers to decorate
wreath, Christmas trees, etc.:

© Disney

Season's Greetings!

To:

From:

© Disney

Merry Christmas!

To:

From:

© Disney

Merry Christmas!

To:

From:

© Disney/Pixar

Happy Holidays!

To:

From:

© Disney

Season's Greetings!

To:

From:

© Disney

Merry Christmas!

To:

From:

© Disney

Happy Holidays!

To:

From:

© Disney

Season's Greetings!

To:

From:

© Disney • Based on the "Winnie the Pooh" works by A. A. Milne and E. H. Shepard

Merry Christmas!

To:

From:

© Disney/Pixar

Happy Holidays!

To:

From:

© Disney